For Börkur

First published in the United States of America in 2005 by Sleeping Bear Press
Text and illustrations copyright © Lani Yamamoto 2005

First published in Great Britain in 2005 by
Frances Lincoln Children's Books, 4 Torriano Mews,
Torriano Avenue, London NW5 2RZ.

Sleeping Bear Press
310 North Main Street, Suite 300
Chelsea, MI 48118
www.sleepingbearpress.com

THOMSON

GALE

©2005 Thomson Gale, a part of the Thomson Corporation.
Thomson and Star Logo are trademarks and Gale and
Sleeping Bear Press are registered trademarks used
herein under license.

Library of Congress Cataloging-in-Publication on file.
ISBN 1-58536-265-4

Printed and bound in Singapore

10 9 8 7 6 5 4 3 2 1

It had been a long day at school

and Albert was happy to be back home.

But before he could finish building his robot,
it was washyourhandsandcomefordinner time.

Then, before he could be rescued from the desert island,
it was inthebathandbrushyourteeth time.

And before the waterfall could finish falling,
it was pyjamasstoryandintobed time.

Everything was moving too fast.

"Stop!" Albert shouted, "Stop, stop, stop, stop!"

Albert would not go to sleep. He was going to stop everything
and do things when HE was ready.

Soon after his parents had gone to bed,
it seemed as if Albert HAD stopped everything.

Albert would not go to sleep. He was going to stop everything
and do things when HE was ready.

Soon after his parents had gone to bed,
it seemed as if Albert HAD stopped everything.

As the world stood silent and still,
Albert watched the night outside his window.

Albert began to think...

These stars have been here since before I was born...

before Mom and Dad were born...

before Grandma and Grandpa were born...

before the dinosaurs were bo...

But before Albert could finish, a star vanished,

and before he could find it again,

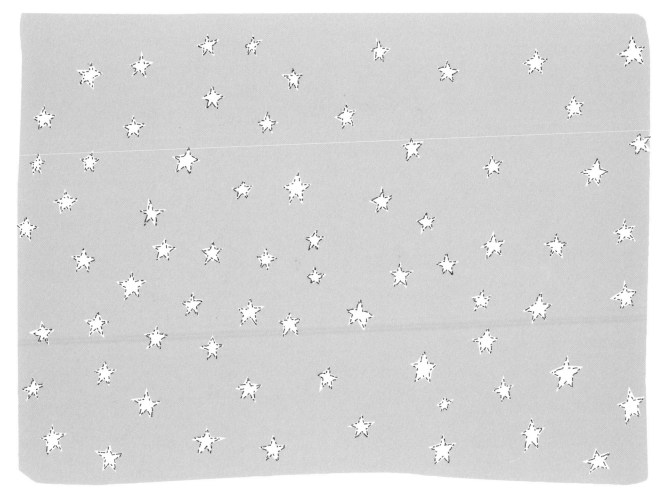

all the stars disappeared into the brightening sky.

Maybe nothing really stops after all,
Albert thought.
Maybe everything is always changing.
Maybe...

But before Albert could finish...

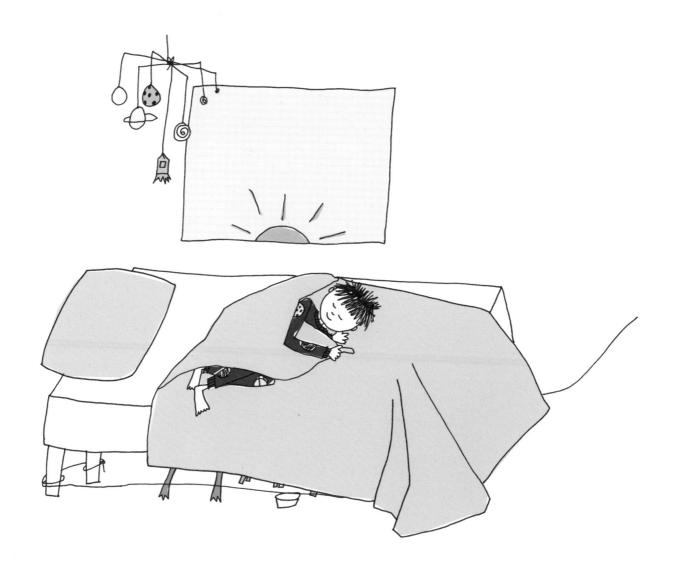